CONTENTS

Also by Jason McBride	v
Introduction	vii
1. Pirate Job Postings	1
2. Secrets In a Bottle	12
3. Pirate Obituaries	23
4. Pirate Love Letters	32
5. Pain and Punishment	42
6. The Daily Life of a Pirate	51
7. Pirate Facts	62
8. Pirate Lies	72
9. Captain's Handbook	81
10. Pirate Classifieds	91
Afterword	101
About the Author	103

PIRATE HAIKU

JASON MCBRIDE

Copyright © 2019 by Jason McBride

All rights reserved.

No part of this book may be reproduced in any form or by any electronic or mechanical means, including information storage and retrieval systems, without written permission from the author, except for the use of brief quotations in a book review.

ALSO BY JASON MCBRIDE

Twisted Haiku Series:

Pirate Haiku

Horror Haiku

Sci-Fi Haiku

Surreal Haiku Zines:

I Stare at the Sea

The Joy of Nothing

Poetry Comics:

Quantum Joy Infinite Melancholy

Wild Divinity

INTRODUCTION

SOME PEOPLE TAKE POETRY VERY SERIOUSLY.

I am not one of those people. If you are a haiku nerd like me, or if you are curious about what Weirdo Poetry is all about, you might enjoy this introduction. But, if that all sounds dull—feel free to skip ahead and read my actual poems. They are dark, twisted, funny, and sometimes disturbing—but they're never boring.

If you are interested in the art of haiku or want an explanation for why I write such strange things, read ahead.

Haiku evolved in Japan from longer forms of poetry over 300 years ago. Haiku focused on nature and the sublime. Traditionally a haiku has 17 *on* (often translated as syllables).

However, a Japanese *on* is different from an English syllable. Haiku were created to be poems you could speak with a single breath. That is tough to do in English.

When haiku came to the West, it was the three lines of five beats or syllables, seven beats, and five beats that caught on. This is how I write my haiku. Many modern poets abandon this form altogether. They write micro-poems that are simply three short lines.

For me, the 17-syllable structure is essential. It forces me to confine my expression. It makes me more creative. Trying to make the 17-syllables work is fun. It's like a puzzle.

Generally, haiku do not rhyme. Most of my haiku do not rhyme, but sometimes I find a rhyme adds an element of whimsy to a particular story.

The three-line structure of haiku is perfect for telling short stories. This is the real reason I write haiku. I love to tell stories.

You can create an intriguing haiku about almost any subject. With haiku, I can drill down to the essential elements of a story. This book is a collection of the haiku-stories I have written about pirates. They are arranged into ten different themes.

In addition to the more than 400 pirate haiku in this collection, there are also a few other types of poems. You will find nonets, hourglass poems, and tanka.

A nonet is a nine-line poem where the first line has nine-syllables, the second line has eight-syllables, and so on until you get to the ninth line, which only has one syllable.

An hourglass poem is a two-stanza poetry form. The first stanza is a nonet. The second stanza is a reverse nonet. It starts with one-syllable and builds to nine-syllables over nine lines. When you center all of the lines, you get an hourglass shape.

A tanka is related to the haiku. It has five lines. The three lines are a standard 5-7-5 haiku with two more lines at the end of seven syllables each.

If after reading this, you still want to read more of my haiku, I publish a new poetry comic every day in my free Weirdo Poetry newsletter. You can subscribe at WeirdoPoetry.Substack.com. You will find a couple of examples of my poetry comics throughout this book. You can also follow me on Twitter (@JasonCMcBride) or Instagram (@weirdo-poetry). There you can read more weird haiku stories. If you get any joy out of this collection of pirate haiku, it would help me out if you could leave a review on whatever platform you bought this book from. Reviews help other keen minds discover my work.

By now, I have weeded out everyone who is not related to me or who isn't as passionate about the possibilities of haiku as I am. I won't keep you any longer.

1
PIRATE JOB POSTINGS

A FTER rummaging through some old papers and artifacts, I found several ancient broadsheets. They were all job advertisements for pirates. Strangely, they were almost all written in haiku. I have reproduced the most interesting ones below.

Help find lost treasure

Keep half of all discovered

Remote position

Is your future bleak?
Entry-level positions
Leave scruples at home

Are you good with birds?
Captain needs parrot minder
Payment D.O.E.

Must have ten fingers
Experience with cannons
Non-smokers preferred

Wanted: New first mate
No previous mutinies
Bring your own pistol

Missing your left hand?
Have extra hook for right mate
Submit references

Pirate Job Postings

Do you love action?
We want you to lead the charge
Entry-level job

Come join world's best crew
Send resume by bottle
Empty the rum first

Ideal candidates
Not troubled by their conscience
Love gold and silver

We are desperate!
Need accurate bookkeeper
Should own gun and sword

Love glory and gold?
Become a pirate today
Must sail your own ship

Adventure awaits
Daily food and grog rations
Space is limited

Need a new ship's cook
Have set of knives in lieu of
Any references

Escape your contract
All of the best pirates were
Indentured servants

Orphans are welcome
Only your mettle matters
Show us what you've got

No inheritance?
Recruiting all second sons
Your future is now

We value your life
Lowest risk of being hanged
Of all major ships

Cause women to swoon
Strike fear in the hearts of men
Be a buccaneer

Handy with a blade?
Eyes in the back of your head?
We need you on board

Find your treasure now!
Join our no obligation
Pirate seminar

Ready to be rich?
Make your own fortune today!
Outcomes may vary

Open position
Ransom Negotiator
Commission only

Wanted: Buccaneer
No background or credit check
At least one tattoo

Seeking rum runner
Asks no questions, have fast ship
We provide cargo

Got legal trouble?
We can get you out of port
Three-year commitment

We love our pirates
Industry best dental plan
Two years-free dentures

Laws are for the weak
Earn your living from the spoils
Of the wretched rich

Tailor, doc, or cook
Expert with needle and thread
Will sew sails and flesh

Allergic to rum?
Seeking new quartermaster
Will train the right fit

Need navigator
With selective memory
Forget on command

Set sail on thirteenth
Superstitious need not join
Rabbit's feet okay

Start-up seeking crew
Prior piracy a plus
Want multitaskers

Simple one time job
Must not believe in curses
Just open a chest

Natural leader?
Take charge of boarding crew
Jobs always open

How high can you climb?
Join our crew as a lookout
Must sleep in crow's nest

You look trustworthy?
On any wanted posters?
Be face of our ship

Seeking brave sailors
Chance for rapid advancement
Incentive payments

You know how to read?
Top crew needs literate mate
May have treasure map

Big, mean, and ugly?
Let's put your talents to work
We always need brutes

Live free on high seas
Join our band of privateers
There's honor in gold

Pirate Resume

Was once Royal Navy cabin boy
Then left her majesty's employ
At our first tropical port
Jumped ship as last resort
Fended for myself
Knowledge? Top shelf
Can climb mast
Run fast
Will
Kill
If you
Tell me too
When weather's grim
Know which sails to trim
Help keep clear of patrols
Navigate the rocky shoals
I'll be your spy amongst the crew
Warn of mutiny—be true to you

Pirate Job Interview

What makes you a good fit for my crew?
Leadership skills and great fighter
You been a pirate before?
Been pillaging for years
Your references?
They're mostly dead
By what cause?
My sword
Bye

2
SECRETS IN A BOTTLE

Before the *Whisper* app, pirates confessed their secrets by writing them on scraps of paper, stuffing them into bottles, and tossing them into the sea. I discovered a bunch of these bottles littering a local beach. Curiously, most of the messages were written in haiku. Here are a few of my favorites.

Got rip-roaring
drunk

Woke up on a
pirate ship

Now, I'm the captain

Fought a Spanish ship
Won a fortune in two hours
Lost it the next night

It was not friendly-
Fire that killed Stephen Hooper
I hated the man

Marooned for three weeks
Before realizing it was
A peninsula

Worst thing anyone
Can say to a proud pirate:
You're a common thief

When the wind won't blow
And the sea is smooth as glass
Death is not far off

More than once
I've fought on both sides of a battle
I can't stand losing

Been on board three years
Still don't know what a jib is
Hopefully luck holds

At night when Peter
Sleeps without his wooden leg
I sand down the end

I got lost looking
For the buried treasure chest
How far is a pace?

Became a pirate
So I could get an earring
Stayed for the parties

My mother still thinks
I'm in a monastery
I did take a vow

Both my eyes are fine
Wear a patch on my left eye
Wanted to fit in

Never trust a man
Without a scar who offers
You fighting advice

Never steal from one
With faster ships or who cares
Less for life than you

Never be the first
To drink, eat, sleep, or get on
Or off of a ship

Plunder is easy
The problem is keeping gold
Pirates all die broke

Simple pirate life:
Plunder, party, lose it all
Set sail and repeat

Find shipmates who are
Dumber and slower than you
You will live longer

I swapped the captain's
Treasure chest with a large trunk
Filled with women's clothes

I'm afraid to tell
Our ship's cook that
I have a shellfish allergy

I hate pillaging
Too much of an introvert
Would rather write songs

Worst cruise of my life
Food is awful Staff is worse
Don't have shuffleboard

Don't trust my crew mates
Might not be getting my share
Should've learned my maths

Most important skill
Is learning to miss meals
Without complaining

More men have perished
From cook's deadly cuisine
Than from cannon blasts

Sought freedom at sea
Pressed into naval service
Joined a pirate crew

What I wouldn't give
For a cabin with a view
And an apple pie

Difference between
Life on a ship and prison:
Can't drown in prison

It takes three days for
An emerald ring to pass
Through a goat's system

Not a real pirate
Joined crew for book research
Now waiting for port

I've gathered more gold
Running rigged dice and card games
Than from any raids

The most popular
Pirates (without enemies)
Tell the best stories

I've got ninety-nine
Problems, but having a job
Sure ain't one of them

Piracy pays more
Than ditch digging and offers
Better benefits

Learned to navigate
By gazing up at the stars
Was drunk, forgot all

The only thing worse
Than an empty rum bottle:
A spilled rum bottle

Stay out of trouble
Tell the same lie so often
You believe it too

Beware old pirates
They have survived and thrived
By betraying friends

Pirates ambush you
They cheat. They lie. They break oaths.
Death doesn't fight fair

I do not fear death
But if it's between me and thee
I will not die first

Best pirate joke starts:
"I once knew a man with a
Wooden leg named Smith."

The most successful
Pirate captains never gained
A reputation

Fighting is risky
Taking flight has better odds
Cowards live longer

Our reputation
For slothful idleness is
Wholly undeserved
It's hard work being
Unrespectable

3
PIRATE OBITUARIES

KNOWING of my current obsession with pirates, a friendly librarian showed me a treasure trove of ancient pirate obituaries. The most remarkable thing about this collection of death notices was that so many of them were written in haiku. The kind curator has allowed me to share a portion of these 17-syllable stories of life and death with you.

Mourning Johnny Smoots

Would've outrun
the hangman

If he'd had two boots

Rum gave him courage
But poor William never had brains
Sharks don't like riders

Cannon Fodder Carl
Thought his nickname was bad luck
Turns out he was right

We loved his footwear
Edmund died with his boots on
Buried without them

Zebediah Jones
Only had one fault. He snored.
Was killed in his sleep

Presumed lost at sea
Paul was fourth to the lifeboat
Only room for three

George learned his lesson
There's no honor among thieves
Only he had any

Captain Francisco
Set adrift by cheering crew
Ran too tight a ship

Walter spoke loudly
Mutiny plans discovered
Made to walk the plank

Rupert only died
Because he was annoying
And the crew was bored

Ralph died with his friends
Funeral well attended
His map still not found

"Eat your vegetables"
Delirious with scurvy
Hugh gave a warning

Some die by the sword
Others perish from gunshots
Thomas choked on lunch

Mark had four aces
Jim had two, and ran Mark through
Mark was the dealer

Samuel swam just fine
But, chained to a cannonball
Proved too hard a test

Too bad Bull Johnson
Found his lost pieces of eight
After he stabbed Ben

"Stronger than ten men",
Big Moose Nelson loved to boast
It only took nine

Pete was our best shot
Said the sleight hurt his honor
Only lost one duel

Jensen was correct
We never could make him talk
But he sure did scream

Squealing on his mates
Saved Robert's long scrawny neck
His house was flammable

Gil tried to go straight
His good deeds did not atone
For much, the judge said

Niles ran slower
Than the ferocious tiger
But faster than Chris

Five men set adrift
Four men were later rescued
Sven had the short straw

Young Bobby Roberts
Never did find his sea legs
We never found him

Rodents chewed the ropes
That once secured the boxes
Which crushed Wesley's spine

Women loved Jasper
Most were betrothed to his mates
His mates hated him

Never did find out
How Rex got stuck underneath
The town's one anvil

How was I to know
We'd need the anchor so soon
After we lashed Red?

It was just Kirk's luck
The one English phrase Francois
Knew was "you bastard"

Bart's gold talisman
Protected him from Voodoo
Not from Syphilis

Frank and Fritz were twins
Frank slept with the captain's girl
Cap' thought it was Fritz

Jude was shot and stabbed
Ignorant of his pardon
Escaping from jail

Bloody Barnaby
Discovered his allergy
To nuts late in life

The storm stole our sails
We devoured our rations
David couldn't fish

No one told Nathan
Don't get a haircut from one
Who owes you money

Reginald survived
Three shipwrecks and a few duels
Not his wife's cooking

Timothy promised
To reverse his evil ways
Killed when church roof fell

Adam was no coward
But if he hadn't been so brave
He'd still be alive

Planned the mutiny
Myles left no detail to chance
Forgot to load gun

Was not the chest wound
That ended Slack-Jaw McGee
The doctor did that

4
PIRATE LOVE LETTERS

For Valentine's Day, a coastal museum displayed the world's most extensive collection of pirate love letters. Most of the scribbles were hard to read. But, I was stunned at how many of these love notes were written in haiku. I dutifully copied down the ones I could make out and have reprinted them below.

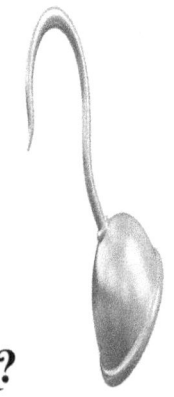

Gazing out at sea

My thoughts turn
to you back home

Did I leave my hook?

Joan's the one for me
Doesn't care what I call her
Name might be Marie

Hope this note finds you
Sent it with the ugliest
Bloke onboard the ship

Watch you with my eye
And wish there was more of me
To love all of you

My man loves me true
He's proud of his pirate gal
If not—run him through

When I saw this ring
I thought of your dainty hands
Snatched it right away

Eyes like the stars
Gentle kisses like the breeze
And rich old parents

If you wanted me
I would give up piracy
But, you love my gold

All my crewmates brag
About some woman from the town
Who's your favorite?

Can't wait to meet you
You're my first pen-pal lover
You're cooking catfish?

What's a man to do
With a mistress and a wife?
Don't mix up the gifts

All the Earth's treasures
Have nothing on your kisses
Love don't pay the bills

Tomorrow a noose
Will stretch out my lying neck
You're my last regret

When leave was over
You never said, "I love you"
Three words and I'd stay

I am not loyal
You can't ever be faithful
If not love, take lust

All I can say is
I love you more than warm rum
Love to have you both

I have one question
Before this goes much farther
You said you're how rich?

If not for silver
I would quit this life for you
But, I'm almost rich

One foot and one hand
Are all that I can offer
I need my one eye

If ours is true love
You will kindly return my
Captain's treasure map

You won't wait for me
I'll carry on without you
Next time we'll start fresh

If this note finds you
I did not live through the night
Enjoy my treasure

Everywhere I go
I am reminded of you
It makes cheating hard

It was either you
Or the bottle. Rum is gone
I made a mistake

The first time we met
You knocked me out with one punch
I'm a lucky man

With every plunder
And with every port town brawl
I'm fighting for you

Our relationship
Status is complicated
I love and you hate

Your love is the wind
I can't stand its full fury
It's calm means my death

You are wine. I'm rum
I am silver to your gold
Never measure up

I love you for you
Not for who your father is
Will take a pardon

While you were away
Another came to steal me
I missed your rum breath

With this note you'll find
One exotic pearl necklace
Doubt you'll send this back

Said I was special
I deserted and returned
Found you two upstairs

First there was anger
Which transformed into hatred
Later you kissed me

I'm not much with words
(More of a man of action)
Is what we have love?

Got your name tattooed
Across my chest right before
I got your letter

Your parents hate me
They say I have no future
But I have your heart

Your eyes are sapphires
Your laugh a bag of gold coins
Your lips are fresh rum

The moment you stole
My last three pieces of eight
I knew we would wed

PAIN AND PUNISHMENT

Below are historical descriptions of the pain and punishment pirates were subjected to. It took a lot of research, but I managed to find several accounts written in haiku. I am in no position to judge the authenticity of these historical sources. But, these pain and punishment vignettes speak for themselves.

Frank went to pieces

His legs were sent
east and west

His arms, north
and south

Hal stole from the boss
We left him buried in sand
Clear up to his neck

The one bite of meat
From the Captain's own table
Was worth the thrashing

Most painful events
Tied to the rack, my first tattoo,
And food poisoning

Dying of thirst and
Watching another drink is
Excruciating

I would rather be
Scourged than hear the first mate eat
He's worse than the bird

Pirates don't have time
To spend torturing captives
Do it anyway

The plank is reserved
For crews with worthless cargo
Slow to surrender

Negotiating
Terms after a mutiny:
Marooned or death now?

Wasn't my victim's
Screams or pleas that bothered me
It was their calm eyes

The first time my cheek
Caught the edge of a steel blade
I knew I was home

Physical wounds heal
But the damage to my soul
Drives me to danger

Of all the places
I've been tortured and beaten
Mom hurt me the most

Captain banned gambling
I bet him it wouldn't take
Swabbed the deck all week

Botched mutiny try
Was tied up to be keel hauled
Boss had heart attack

My only regret
About sleeping on duty
Is in getting caught

Knew a man who cut
Straight through his hand to escape
He died of blood loss

Was branded by the
East India Company
Wasn't pirate yet

Food rations ran out
Cooked-up the captain's parrot
Was lashed to the mast

Is Chinese water
Torture real or just a myth?
About to find out

Pirate brain twister:
Does it hurt more to lose your
Hand, foot, or your eye?

Terror is stronger
Than steel and more explosive
Than packed gunpowder

I've received more scars
From the navy and the law
Than I ever gave

Sticks and stones may break
Bones—call me a name and I will
Cut you to pieces

I'm not scared of pain
It's the only sensation
That I can still feel

A priest once asked me
Why I wasn't scared of Hell
I'm already there

I prefer the stocks
Over thumbscrews. But a good
Thrashing is faster

First our food was gone
Then our water. Last we lost
Our humanity

I broke my mum's heart
When I left home at thirteen
Never forgave me

Local constable
Sobered me up in jail cell
While he played bugle

I'd rather cross a
Hanging judge than fail to pay
My bar tab in port

I can suffer pain
But do not make me listen
To the cook's singing

No torture corrects
Behavior as quickly as
Withholding of rum

Taking Will's leg was
Less of a punishment and
More morale booster

If ever captured I know
I face the gallows
Won't go peacefully

No man is a law
Unto himself, except for
Thayne, he's enormous

You can get away
With almost anything if
You can stand the lash

Locked up in a cell
Can hear and smell the ocean
Never sail again

Decapitation—
Our smiling interpreter
Relayed the chief's words

The only warning
Pirate corpses on pikes give
Is do not get caught

6
THE DAILY LIFE OF A PIRATE

One untapped resource for pirate researchers and enthusiasts are the caches of pirate journals and diaries found in many of the world's great libraries. Those most familiar with the pirate sub-culture will not be surprised to learn that many entries detailing the daily struggles of life on the sea were written in haiku.

Women not allowed

To captain in
the navy

So I turned pirate

Boarded a big ship
Liberated the cargo
Was shipment of stones

Nobody told me
Piracy was so boring
Catch more rats than gold

The smell of blood and
Gunpowder is both thrilling
And terrifying

When you are loyal
Only to yourself, you die
Free and all alone

First day with a new
Captain is the best sailing
Next day is the worst

The Daily Life of a Pirate

The ladies never
Seem to mind my smell until
I run out of gold

Get paid not to steal
Pirate retirement plan
No employer match

Dear Journal: Today
I drank all my rum rations
Not a hint of wind

Got my share of loot
Landed with a bag of gold
Returned with no pants

Gave chase in the straits
Crafty sea dogs out ran us
I won my wager

My best sleep in weeks
Was rudely interrupted
Was on watch duty

Almost lost my life
Nothing is more dangerous
Than idle pirates

My turn to be flogged
Not sure what the offense was
Need to stop drinking

Life of Pirate Pearl:
I went to sea a captive
Came back a captain

Out ran a frigate
Held a whole town for ransom
All in a day's work

Day seventy-five
Rescue now seems unlikely
I hate coconuts

Sentence was pronounced.
"Was just following orders."
Didn't impress judge

Spent all our powder
In some brutal fusillades
Was all friendly fire

Began studying
Market inefficiencies
Planning next attack

Another tattoo
Finally spelled my name right
Czech pirate problems

Serendipity
Has not yet favored us with
Any of her charms

Gold flows like water
When we come to port loaded
Who are the pirates?

Joined as cabin boy
Saw the world, became a man
Left to find a wife

Was bored one evening
Made a few fake treasure maps
Put them in bottles

Fighting with honor
Is the ideal of men who
Have not been to war

The Daily Life of a Pirate

Pressed into navy
Jumped ship, became a pirate
Pressed back in navy

Mothers never let
Your babies grow up to be
Customs officials

Spent five nights at sea
For every night spent on land
Hope I die at sea

Discovered my son
Never knew he existed
He wants to kill me

Sometimes I believe
I would have made a great priest
Than I drink more rum

An old hand told me
The key to staying alive
Is don't volunteer

The only thing worse
Than running out of rations
Is eating on ship

Kept a souvenir
From every one of my kills
Have a seagull beak

The sea will provide
Food, shelter, clothing, and wealth
Inside other ships

The Daily Life of a Pirate

Lost a bet today
Waiting for another raid
Need a new peg leg

Men accepted me
As their equal once I shot
Captain and first mate

The worst sound at sea
Is the sound of snoring from
One of your crewmates

My two favorite days
Are when we arrive in port
And when we depart

I once got so drunk
I got on board the wrong ship
Nobody noticed

When I quit sailing
I'll finally write my book
Once I learn to read

Ferocious battle
We offered them no quarter
I watched from hiding

Scanning horizon
Watching for ships, land, or storms
Anxious for what's next

A short life at sea
Of risk and debauchery
Better than long life
Of sobriety
And toil on land

Are pirates scumbags
Or victims of a system
With few options for
Social advancement
And stable wages?

The Daily Life of a Pirate

Was once privateer
A brave and bold patriot
Without my consent
Peace treaty was signed
Now I'm a pirate

PIRATE FACTS

Few characters have suffered more from historical misinformation than the pirate. I have surveyed all the reputable scholarly sources on buccaneers, and all of the surviving original sources. From these, I have pulled fascinating, authentic glimpses into pirate life, many of which happen to be formulated as haiku.

One well placed
bribe skirts

Countless acts
of violence

Corruption
saves lives

Pirate Facts

It's only a crime
If you get caught or someone
Snitches to the Crown

Bravest man on board
Is the first to taste a meal
From an angry cook

Pirates go to sea
Not for jewels, gold, or silver.
They go to be free

Pirates were the first
Multi-level marketers
Tupperware with swords

How many bottles
Of rum equals mutiny?
Simple pirate math

When saved by pirates
Part company before they
No longer need you

There is more treasure
In the port's bars and brothels
Than in any ship

More pirates have been
Killed because of rats than by
The Royal Navy

Out of all the knots
Only the noose ever gets
Pirates in trouble

Pirates only drink
To drown their consciences or
Stifle their boredom

Pirates wouldn't steal
If the Queen would allow them
To collect taxes

Famous pirate myth:
All pirates do is drink rum
False. They drink wine too

Dead men tell no tales
But, their loved ones are often
Very talkative

Pirates were start-ups
Some bootstrapped, others needed
Venture Capital

Murder and mayhem
Are only byproducts of
Our treasure hunting

Personal hygiene
Is a luxury pirates
Have no interest in

Pure democracy
Was found on pirate vessels
Not legislatures

Analyzing risk:
Actuaries and pirates
Overlapping skills

The hold is getting full
Stray ship on the horizon
Time for an upgrade

Opportunity
Matters more than any plan
Be ready to act

The lowest form of
Self-destructive behavior
Is turning pirate

Pirates pillage ships
Royals pillage whole countries
Who's the criminal?

Big one got away
Piracy is like fishing
Most the time you wait

No worse luck at sea
Than to spot a fast moving
Ship of mad pirates

Pirates love to sing
Nobody loves to hear them
This is why they drink

We don't swashbuckle
We surprise our victims with
Overwhelming force

Pirate life swings from
Extreme deprivation to
Base depravity

World's best pirate
Was a Chinese concubine
Got paid to go straight

Each man has one vote
And equal share of the loot
Per the pirate code

Not cannons or swords
Most potent weapon is fear
True pirate secret

The sun is our clock
The night sky is our theater
The sea is our grave

More wealth will pass through
Any pair of banker's hands
Than through a pirate's

The fine line between
Patriot and pirate is
Crossed for small profits

Pirates can't go straight
Not because they covet gold
They covet freedom

We steal openly
Bureaucrats steal secretly
Who is more honest?

Buccaneers don't fret
O'er what lurks in the unknown
They're scared of what's known

We dream of lovers
We will never truly know
We're bound to the sea

Wealth is made on land
The desperate go to sea
Pirates are hopeless

Every pirate knows
Life will end bloody or at
The end of a rope

Honest pirates and
Honest fortune tellers are
Awful at their jobs

―――

We drink too much rum
For there to be any chests
Of gold to bury

―――

We're only brave when
We outnumber enemies
More than five to one

―――

Pirate's golden rule
Seize the gold by any means
Spend the gold quickly
Live rich on land
Back to sea when broke

―――

Death is violence
Stabbed, shot, drowned, disemboweled
Hanged, poisoned, or burnt
Leads to same place as
Disease and old age

PIRATE LIES

One of the most enduring and endearing qualities of a skilled pirate is his or her ability to lie. Pirate lies are some of the most exciting tales you will find. The greatest liars put their deceptions into haiku.

I've never stolen

Anything from anyone

It's all donations

Had other options
Chose not to attend Oxford
Just wanted to sail

Time for me to go
Set sail early tomorrow
This is my last drink

Suspicious cargo?
'Course I have the paperwork
Let me go fetch it

I live by the rule
Always tell the truth, damn
The consequences

No. You don't know me
Just have one of those faces
My first time at sea

My word is my bond
I'd rather die than speak lies
You've heard what before?

There is no problem
I could stop at any time
Drink rum for my health

I am no pirate
They kidnapped me from my ship
Would never desert

I have no idea
How your portion of plunder
Got in my locker

Lockjaw Jim and I
Went ashore together, he
Had an accident

Pirate Lies

Surrender right now
And no harm will come to you
It's strictly business

Nothing could make me snitch
On any fellow shipmates
Not gold nor pardon

You're my only girl
In other ports I never
Even leave the ship

What other woman?
That letter is from Mother
She's affectionate

You are my true love
Those other girls mean nothing
Jenny's not your name?

Hey! Man overboard!
Johnny and I have had our rows
I tried to save him

I thought you were dead
I was going to send your boots
To your family

You're faster than me
But, I am the better shot
You go, I'll cover

I swear on the life
Of my dear sweet grandmother
I don't cheat at cards

I don't even know
How to rig a game of chance
Double or nothing?

'Course I have a plan
But I don't want to ruin
The surprise ahead

Dearest Mum and Dad
I was just made the first mate
Of our merchant ship

Go help the captain
We will hold the lifeboat here
It's the pirate code

I trust my crewmates
There is honor among thieves
I have no secrets

I would love to help
But I never got to see
Where the gold was hid

Why would I take
Your golden tooth while you slept?
Maybe it fell out

I know what happened
To everyone's rum rations
The rats drank it all

We are the victims
Pirates stole all our cargo
Ignore those cannons

We rescued these goods
There is no bill of lading
Just helping a friend

If I had any
I would gladly share with you
Just drank my last drop

Pirate Lies

I would've come back
But I was grievously
Injured in battle

Would I lie to you?
So, Babette is your sister?
Maybe she's jealous

You scared me to death
Me? I'm not sneaking around
Was just sleepwalking

Can't swab the deck now
Much too sick. Must be scurvy
Stand up and I'll die

I'm quick to obey
Never have to tell me twice
I'll get right to it

Cook swears it's chicken
No one's seen a rat for days
Some coincidence

Only savages
Practice cannibalism
The sharks were too fierce

The compact is clear
Your share is seven percent
Sorry you can't read

Who me? Mutiny?
Not even sure what that is
You're a great captain

9
CAPTAIN'S HANDBOOK

Sometimes the most striking artifacts were originally the most banal objects. I came across a handbook for pirate captains. Its pages were filled with useful tips about everything from accounting to ship discipline. The most crucial instructions were written in haiku. I have reproduced some of the gems I uncovered.

Micromanaging
Won't get the deck
swabbed faster
A well placed
lash does

Booze, women, and cards
Best pirate recruiting tools
Come with downsides

Popular first mates
Are a captain's biggest threat
Better watch your back

When two men squabble
Resolve the dispute quickly
Punish everyone

Keys to discipline:
Frequent public punishment
Secret, private praise

There's only one bond
Strong enough to tie your crew
To your command: Fear

Your crew needs to know
No man is so important
That you won't kill him

Find the smartest man
Kick him off of your ship
Brains equal trouble

Always mind your tongue
The crew becomes angry when
Called cannon fodder

When culling the crew
Don't leave family members
Who can plot revenge

Every captain needs
At least two spies in the crew
To report on plots

Learn to delegate
Never do your own whipping
Much too dangerous

Both too many friends
Or too many enemies
On board equals death

If all of them die
Who will spread fear and panic?
Must leave a witness

Respect the cowards
They will survive the longest
Won't lead mutinies

No self-respecting
Pirate captain would ever
Go down with the ship

The captain who counts
On loyalty from the crew
Only sets sail once

Show me a captain
With no secrets from the crew
I will show you bones

Never trust someone
Who out-drinks or out-thinks you
On board your vessel

If rations run out
Stage an execution of
The quartermaster

Remember your crew
Is only happy until
All the grog is gone

Write logbook in code
Keep the cipher on shore
Don't forget the code

When it comes to cooks
Loyalty outweighs their skill
Don't die from poison

Always have a dog
They're more loyal than parrots
Will try your food first

You're not paranoid
Everyone does want you dead
Captains have no friends

Supernatural
Forces cannot be controlled
Do not trust in them

Always be ready
To blame a despised crewman
For a bad omen

Busy crews don't plot
Swab the decks, balance cargo,
And repair the sails

Do not waste good rope
On torture or on murder
Throw men overboard

Hold ten percent back
Of the men's share when in port
Keep it if they die

A man's dying wish
Should be honored unless it
Is inconvenient

When it comes to ships
Speed is more important than
Size, guns, or beauty

Inspire your crew
With creative punishments
True leaders are feared

Two worst offences:
One, insubordination
Two, theft from captain

If you hear whispers
Assume mutiny is neigh
Escape or defend

Most first time captains
Are killed within a few months
Most by their own crews

Three ways out for you:
Painful death, royal pardon
Deserted island

If you can't answer
A crewman's question, flog them
You are all knowing

If you fail to kill
Someone periodically
You will lose your edge

Maintaining morale
Requires both rum and lies
Don't lie about rum

10
PIRATE CLASSIFIEDS

The black market was more than just a place to move goods of dubious origin and legitimacy. It was also a place to find rare items, shop for gifts, and procure services. Those in the know would often post ads in a secret underground newspaper. It was the Craigslist of the buccaneer set. While few copies of this black market classified section survived, I managed to find a partial edition. Strangely, most of the ad copy was drafted in haiku.

Used glass eye for sale
Beautiful. Looks almost real
Owner has moved on

Bird needs loving home
Curses in six languages
Parrot prefers rum

Deluxe, large strongbox
Locked. The key is lost. You must
Dispose of body

Seeking a left hook
Must be new or gently used
Must not have blood stains

Have handsome dentures
Handcrafted of ivory
They leave deep bite marks

Easily concealed
Handmade shiv—great in dungeons
Carved from my wrist bone

Looking for cannons?
New ship has too many guns
Cannons sold as is

Embellished chess set
Only missing single pawn
Couldn't dislodge it

Twenty-one foot skiff
Fast ship. Bare bones. No cannons.
Starboard side has hole

One case of cheap rum
Contact the Royal Navy
This is not a trap

Full set of silver
Once owned by a French bishop
Perfect for parties

Need some extra coin?
Help ambush your vessel
Gold and great story

Large ring collection
All currently still attached
To owner's fingers

Set of voodoo dolls
You must possess black magic
Will discuss targets

Need a special gift?
Try exotic shrunken heads
No two are alike

Need skillful locksmith
Willing to unlock shackles
Asking for a friend

Have lucky bracelet
Only selling because of
Recent loss of arms

Used cat-o-nine tails
Ideal for getting answers
From reluctant tongues

Coded treasure map
You must decipher yourself
Leave contact info

Vintage looking glass
Recovered from merchant wreck
Sell or trade. Name price

Are your initials: TSJ?
Buy monogrammed cutlass
Engraver's mistake

Need a miracle
Looking for caskets of wine
Will trade fresh water

Gorgeous hand drawn map
Details pubs, inns, and taverns
Around Port Royal

Willing to work for
Quick passage to Tortuga
Ship left without me

Missing new glass eye
Lost it during rum fueled fight
Please return to Pete

Don't get lost again
Full set of nautical charts
Some minor bloodstains

Chinese hand cannon
Tough to aim, slow to reload
Works well as club

My special report
Port officials who take bribes
In Caribbean

Bespoke captain's gear
Pillage and plunder in style
Fashion Buccaneer

Need quarantine flag?
Best deterrent to boarding
Keep customs at bay

Vintage glass bottles
Once held world's finest rum
Trade for full bottles

Three sets of earrings
Each one thick solid gold hoop
My mother said no

Have hold full of tea
Will sell to highest bidder
Must unload tonight

Selection of silks
Recently liberated
From crooked merchants

Genuine pardons
East India Company
Just fill in the blank

No luck with ladies?
Try one of our love potions
Guaranteed to work

You'll be popular
With this compact DIY
Pirate tattoo kit

Buy shark repellant
Improve your odds next shipwreck
One per customer

Deluxe lock pick set
Get into any treasure
Out of any cell

Don't leave it to fate
World's largest selection
Of good luck totems

Before you set sail
Set your affairs in order
Custom pirate wills

Get your copy of
The Pirate Captain's Handbook
Comes with free eye patch

AFTERWORD

Thank you for reading *Pirate Haiku*. Believe it or not, convincing people to buy and read a book about pirate poetry is tough. If you enjoyed this book, it would help me out if you would leave a review on the platform where you purchased this book.

Reviews help other smart and discerning readers find this book in a crowded marketplace. Reviews can also help persuade people who are the fence about investing their coffee money on some crazy haiku collection.

If you love haiku as much as I do, you will love my free daily newsletter, Weirdo Poetry. I publish a new poetry comic every day. You can check it out at WeirdoPoetry.Substack.com. I regularly publish haiku on topics as diverse as time travel, the coming robot uprising, fairy tales, and how to avoid being productive at work.

If you subscribe to my newsletter, you will also be the first to know about book releases and other new projects.

ABOUT THE AUTHOR

Jason McBride is a writer, poet, collage artist, and illustrator. He also publishes a daily poetry comic newsletter called Weirdo Poetry.

He is the author of two full haiku collections, two haiku zines, an illustrated collection of prose poems, and a collection of haiku comics.

twitter.com/WeirdoPoetry
instagram.com/weirdo_poetry

www.ingramcontent.com/pod-product-compliance
Lightning Source LLC
LaVergne TN
LVHW012028060526
838201LV00061B/4510